Peppa Pig™

Peppa Plays Football

It's a sunny day and Peppa Pig and
Suzy Sheep are playing tennis.
"To you, Suzy!" cheers Peppa, hitting
the ball. Now it's Suzy's turn.
"To you, Peppa!" she cries, hitting the ball
straight over Peppa's head. Oh dear!

"Waaaa!" George feels a bit left out.

"Sorry, George," says Peppa. "You can't play tennis. We only have two racquets."

"George can be the ball boy!" cheers Suzy.

"Being a ball boy is a very important job, George," says Peppa.

Peppa and Suzy are having lots of fun,
but they keep missing the ball.
"Ball boy!" they shout together.
"Huff, puff!" George is not having fun.
He keeps running to get the ball and
he is very tired!

"Hello, everyone," cries Peppa when her
friends arrive. "We're playing tennis."
"Can we play too?" asks Danny Dog.
"There aren't enough racquets,"
replies Suzy Sheep.

"Let's play football then," says Danny Dog. "Football! Hooray!" everyone cheers.

"We can play girls against boys," says Peppa.

"Each team needs a goalkeeper," says Danny Dog.

"Me, me!" shouts Pedro Pony.

"Me, me!" cries Rebecca Rabbit.

Pedro Pony and Rebecca Rabbit
decide to be the goalkeepers.
"The boys' team will start!" says Danny Dog.
Richard Rabbit gets the ball and runs
very fast, right by Peppa Pig,
Suzy Sheep and Candy Cat
and straight up to the . . .

. . . "GOAL!" cry Danny and Pedro together,
as Richard Rabbit kicks the ball straight
past Rebecca Rabbit and into the net.
"The boy is a winner!" cheers Danny Dog.
"That's not fair, we weren't ready," moans Peppa.

Rebecca Rabbit picks up the ball and runs.
"Hey!" shouts Danny Dog.
"That's cheating! You can't hold the ball."
"Yes I can!" says Rebecca. "I'm the goalkeeper."
Rebecca throws the ball into the goal,
straight past Pedro Pony.
"GOAL!" she cries.

"That goal is not allowed," says Pedro.

"Yes, it is," says Peppa.

"No, it isn't!" barks Danny.

"What a lot of noise," snorts Daddy Pig.

"I'll be the referee.

The next team to get a goal will win the game."

Richard Rabbit and George run off with the football, while everyone is still talking.
"Where's the ball?" asks Peppa.
But it's too late! Richard Rabbit kicks the ball straight into the goal, past Pedro Pony.
"Hooray! The boys win!" cries Danny.

"Football is a silly game," sighs Peppa, disappointed.
"Just a moment," says Daddy Pig. "The boys scored
in their own goal, that means the girls win!"
"Really?" gasp all the girls. "Hooray!"
"Football is a great game!" cheers Peppa.
"Ha, ha, ha!" everyone laughs.